DUSTBIN DAD

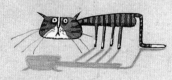

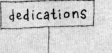

dedications

For Mum and Dad
PB
For Mum and Dad
RA

SIMON AND SCHUSTER
First published in Great Britain in 2013
by Simon and Schuster UK Ltd
1st Floor, 222 Gray's Inn Road, London WC1X 8HB
A CBS Company

imprint Stuff

Text copyright © 2013 Peter Bently
Illustrations copyright © 2013 Russell Ayto
The right of Peter Bently and Russell Ayto to be identified
as the author and illustrator of this work has been asserted
by them in accordance with the Copyright, Designs and
Patents Act, 1988
A CIP catalogue record for this book is available from
the British Library upon request
978-1-84738-873-5 (HB)
978-1-84738-874-2 (PB)
978-0-85707-900-8 (eBook)
Printed in China
1 3 5 7 9 10 8 6 4 2

DUSTBIN DAD

title

dustbin

dad

PETER BENTLY

author

and RUSSELL AYTO

illustrator

SIMON AND SCHUSTER
London   New York   Sydney   Toronto   New Delhi

Unfinished sandwiches,

cold soggy fries,

unwanted broccoli,

half-eaten pies.

Tomatoes with toothmarks,

odd scraps of fish,

crunchy bits left on the side
of the dish.

Clammy spaghetti,

the whites of boiled eggs —

'Your father,' says Mum,

'is
a
dustbin
on
legs.'

Now, we have a cat named Amelia Scrimp –
she's sweet but, quite frankly, a bit of a wimp.

'That mog,' said the vet, 'needs some Puss-Pep-Up-Powder.

You mix it with water.

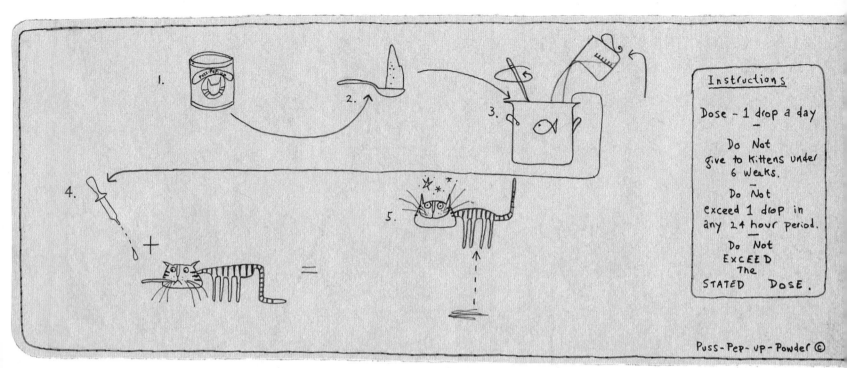

It tastes like fish chowder.

One droplet will perk up your puss-cat like heck.

'I seem to be sprouting a gingery beard!'

Then he gasped as his hands became glomping great paws, and his fingernails turned into needle-sharp claws!

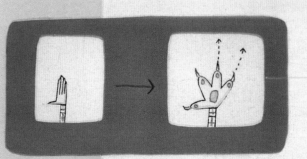

He started to quiver.
He started to quail.
Then out of the back of his
pants popped –

a tail!
That potion was potent,
no doubt about that.
My dad had turned into a gigantic ...

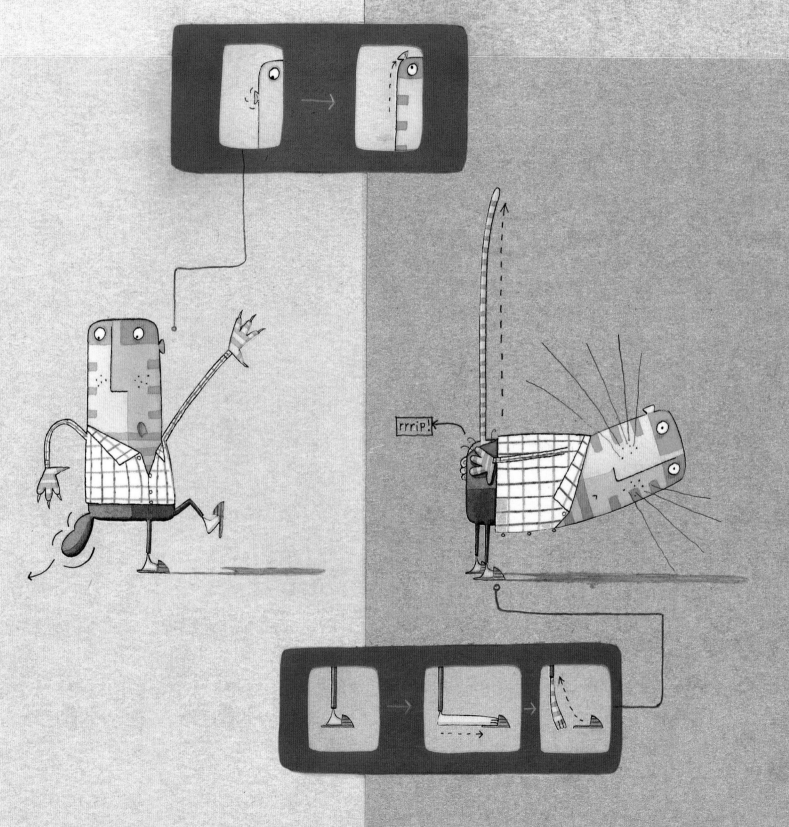

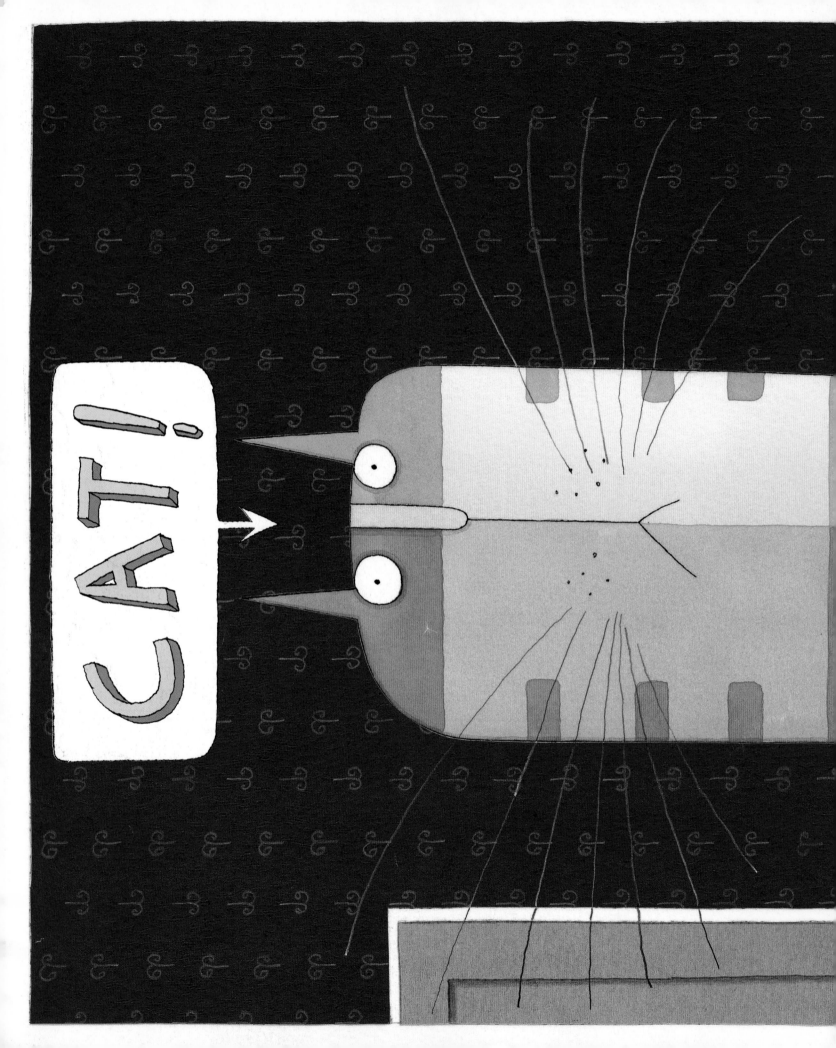

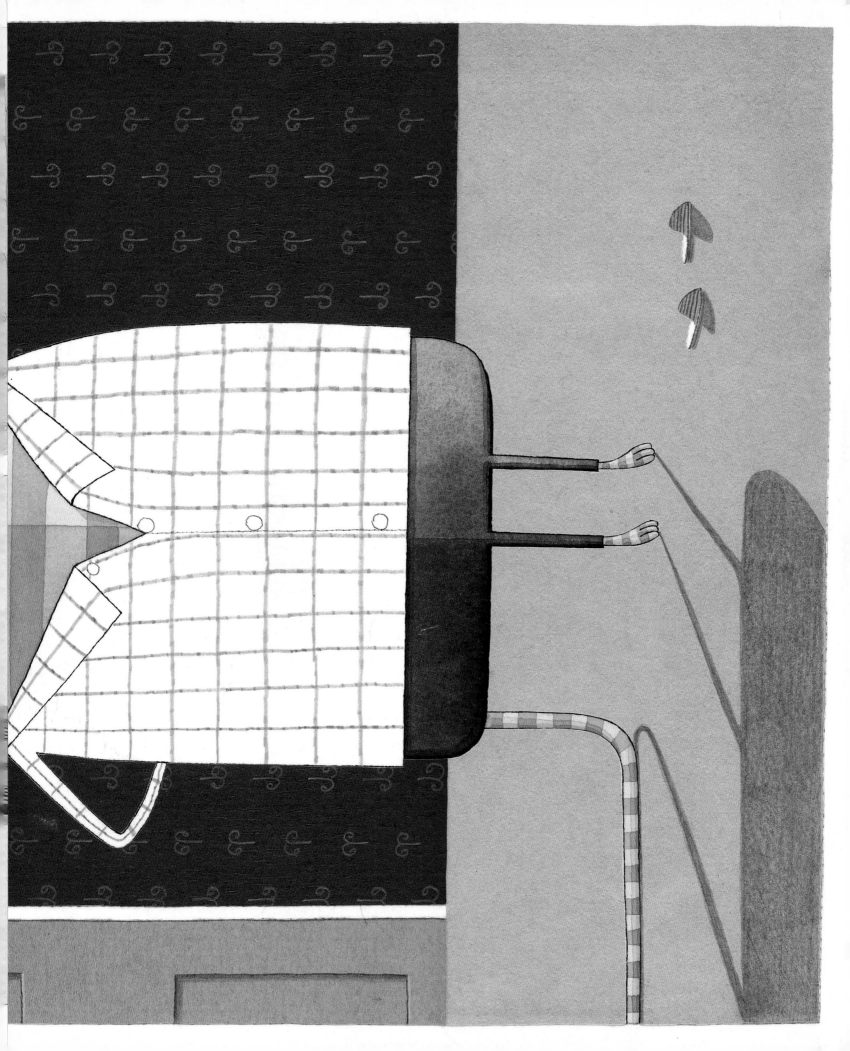

He pounced on –

and swallowed –

a
very
large
bug,

and
totally
trashed
our new table and rug.

He licked himself clean with a satisfied purr.

Then –

Hack!

Hack!

HACK!

– coughed up a large ball of fur.

He trampled the blooms
of our neighbour, Miss Hawn,
and I just can't describe
what he left on her lawn . . .

poo

Miss Hawn shouted, 'Shoo!'
from her kitchen, then . . .

'GOSH!' we all gasped,
as my Dad went

miaaaaaoooooooo

He fell in the rubbish.
What clatter and din!

Then we heard a loud  coming out of the bin.

Dad had
changed back
again,
quick as a flash,

and stood, quite bewildered,
in yesterday's trash.

'What happened?' he groaned.
'Am I dreaming? Or mad?'

'No,' declared Mum.

'Just
a
REAL
Dustbin
Dad.'

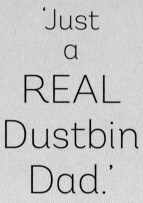

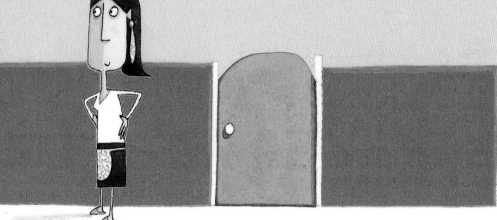

So, **never** leave food where your father can grab it.
He's likely to start up a scrap-eating habit.

Then he, too, might suffer a similar fate–

unless you eat ALL of the food on your plate!